Incy Wincy Spider

and other nursery rhymes

illustrated by VALERIA PETRONE

It's raining, it's pouring,
The old man is snoring;
He went to bed,
And bumped his head,
And couldn't get up in the
morning.

Published by Ladybird Books Ltd
80 Strand London WC2R 0RL
A Penguin Company
11 13 15 17 19 20 18 16 14 12
© LADYBIRD BOOKS LTD MCMXCIV
This edition MCMXCIX

Printed in Italy

Incy Wincy spider
Climbed up the spout;
Down came the rain
And washed the spider out.

Out came the sunshine
And dried up all the rain;
Incy Wincy spider
Climbed the spout again.

Three blind mice,
Three blind mice,
See how they run,
See how they run!
They all ran after
   the farmer's wife,
Who cut off their tails
   with a carving knife,
Did you ever see such
   a thing in your life,
As three blind mice?

Pussy cat, Pussy cat,
   where have you been?
"I've been up to London
   to look at the Queen."
Pussy cat, Pussy cat,
   what did you there?
"I frightened a little mouse
   under her chair."

Ride a cock-horse to Banbury Cross,
To see a fine lady upon a white horse;
With rings on her fingers
    and bells on her toes,
She shall have music
    wherever she goes.

Cock-a-doodle-doo!
My dame has lost her shoe,
My master's lost his
    fiddling stick,
And doesn't know
    what to do.

Polly, put the kettle on,
Polly, put the kettle on,
Polly, put the kettle on,
 We'll all have tea.

Sukey, take it off again,
Sukey, take it off again,
Sukey, take it off again,
 They've all gone away.

Little Tommy Tucker,
Sings for his supper:
What shall we give him?
White bread and butter.
How will he cut it
Without a knife?
How will he marry
Without a wife?

"Oranges and lemons,"
Say the bells of St Clement's.

"You owe me five farthings,"
Say the bells of St Martin's.

"When will you pay me?"
Say the bells of Old Bailey.

"When I grow rich,"
Say the bells of Shoreditch.

"Pray, when will that be?"
Say the bells of Stepney.

"I'm sure I don't know,"
Says the great bell at Bow.

Here comes a candle
To light you to bed.
Here comes a chopper
To chop off your head.

See-saw, Margery Daw,
Johnny shall have
a new master;
He shall have
but a penny a day,
Because he can't work any faster.

Georgie Porgie, pudding and pie,
Kissed the girls
and made them cry;
When the boys
came out to play,
Georgie Porgie ran away.

Jack and Jill went up the hill
To fetch a pail of water;
Jack fell down and broke his crown,
And Jill came tumbling after.

Up Jack got, and home did trot,
As fast as he could caper,
He went to bed to mend his head,
With vinegar and brown paper.

Round and round the garden
Like a teddy bear;
One step, two step,
Tickle you under there!

Here am I,
Little Jumping Joan;
When nobody's with me,
I'm all alone.

Jack be nimble,
Jack be quick,
Jack jump over
    the candlestick.

Dickery, dickery, dare,
The pig flew up in the air;
The man in brown
Soon brought him down,
Dickery, dickery, dare.

17

Hush-a-bye, baby,
on the tree top,
When the wind blows,
the cradle will rock.
When the bough breaks,
the cradle will fall,
Down will come baby,
cradle and all.

I had a little nut tree,
Nothing would it bear
But a silver nutmeg
And a golden pear.

The King of Spain's daughter
Came to visit me,
And all for the sake
Of my little nut tree.

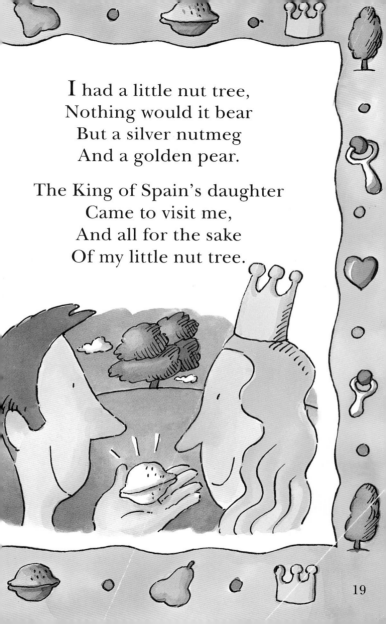

19

This little pig went to market,
This little pig stayed at home,
This little pig had roast beef,
This little pig had none,
And this little pig cried: *"Wee-wee-wee,"*
All the way home.

Tom, Tom, the piper's son,
Stole a pig and away did run;
The pig was eat
And Tom was beat,
And Tom went howling
  down the street.

To market, to market, to buy a fat pig,
Home again, home again, jiggety jig;
To market, to market, to buy a fat hog,
Home again, home again, jiggety jog.

Pease porridge hot,
Pease porridge cold,
Pease porridge in the pot,
Nine days old.
Some like it hot,
Some like it cold,
Some like it in the pot,
Nine days old.

Half a pound of tuppenny rice,
Half a pound of treacle;
That's the way the money goes –
Pop goes the weasel!

Hot cross buns!
Hot cross buns!
One a penny, two a penny,
Hot cross buns!
If you have no daughters,
Give them to your sons,
One a penny, two a penny,
Hot cross buns!

Pat-a-cake, pat-a-cake, baker's man,
Bake me a cake, as fast as you can;
Pat it and prick it and mark it with B,
And put it in the oven for baby and me.

Little Boy Blue,
Come blow your horn,
The sheep's in the meadow,
The cow's in the corn.
But where is the boy
Who looks after the sheep?
"He's under a haycock,
Fast asleep."
Will you wake him?
"No, not I,
For if I do,
He's sure to cry."

Diddle, diddle, dumpling,
my son John,
Went to bed
with his trousers on;
One shoe off,
and one shoe on,
Diddle, diddle, dumpling,
my son John.

There was an old woman
   tossed up in a basket,
Seventeen times as high as the moon;
Where she was going
   I couldn't but ask her,
For in her hand she carried a broom.
"Old woman, old woman, old woman,"
   quoth I,
"Where are you going to up so high?"
To brush the cobwebs off the sky!
"May I go with you?"
Yes, by-and-by.

Notes on nursery rhymes
by Geraldine Taylor (Reading Consultant)

Collections of nursery rhymes are among the first books we share with babies and children. Each rhyme is an exciting story with song and action.

Nursery rhymes have a vital impact on early learning and they are a traditional part of childhood happiness for everyone.

Early skills
There's evidence that nursery rhymes help to develop the skills needed for reading, spelling and number. Rhyme and word-play help children to recognise sounds and stimulate language development. Feeling and beating rhythm and hearing counting rhymes encourage early number ideas.